WHO KILLED MR. BODDY?

Look for these books in the
Clue® series:

Clue®

WHO KILLED MR. BODDY?

Book created by A. E. Parker

Written by Eric Weiner

Based on characters from the Parker Brothers game

A Creative Media Applications Production

SCHOLASTIC INC.
New York Toronto London Auckland Sydney

Special thanks to: Thomas Dusenberry,
Julie Ryan, Laura Millhollin, Sandy Upham,
Jean Feiwel, Greg Holch, Dona Smith,
Nancy Smith, John Simko, and Elizabeth Parisi.

ISBN 0-590-46110-9

12 11 10 9 8 7 6 5 4 3 2   2 3 4 5 6 7/9
                                                          40

Printed in the U.S.A.
First Scholastic printing, August 1992

For Bob Stewart

Contents

WHO KILLED MR. BODDY?

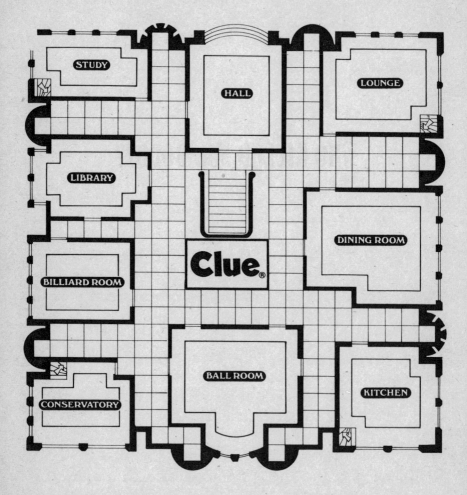

Allow Me To Introduce Myself . . .

MY NAME IS REGINALD BODDY, AND I'M your host for the weekend. I trust you'll find your stay here at my mansion a most comfortable one. And I do hope that this time there won't be a murder!

Oh, please don't be upset. It's just that I have these other guests staying here as well, and . . . well, it seems that whenever these six people get together, there's always a bit of trouble.

Don't get me wrong. My friends usually get along marvelously. Of course, there was the time that Mr. Green tried to club Professor Plum with the Wrench in the Billiard Room. But everyone argues from time to time, right?

Actually, you can help me out. Sort of keep an eye out, would you? Look for clues. That way, if something does happen — a ghastly, horrifying crime, say — you could tell me who did it.

You have only six suspects to worry about. (I, of course, will never be a suspect!) The six suspects are:

Mr. Green: A fine businessman, but a bit of a bully, I'm afraid. His bark is worse than his bite. Unfortunately, I've experienced both.

Colonel Mustard: A dashing gallant, ready to fight a duel at the drop of a hat. So be careful not to drop your hat.

Mrs. Peacock: There isn't a single bad word one could say about this good-hearted woman. Why? Because she's so prim and proper, she won't allow anyone to say a single bad word!

Professor Plum: A good man, but a tad forgetful. He once forgot he was talking to me in the middle of a sentence!

Miss Scarlet: A beautiful woman, as anyone will tell you. Why, Miss Scarlet will tell you herself.

Mrs. White: My loyal maid. She has served me happily and faithfully for years. I'm sure that the poison in my coffee was just an honest mistake.

Don't worry. I'll give you a chart of the suspects, weapons, and rooms at the end of each mystery. As you read, you can check off the suspects until you've narrowed your list down to one.

And now, if you'll excuse me, I must be going. I, er, just heard a bloodcurdling scream coming from the . . . Conservatory. . . .

1.
Who Killed Pitty-Pat?

IN THE CONSERVATORY, MRS. WHITE let out a bloodcurdling scream. Her hands clutched the lace collar of her maid's uniform. Her face twisted with terror.

"Good heavens!" cried Mr. Boddy, running into the room. "What is it?"

She pointed downward. At her feet lay a mass of green feathers.

"Oh, no!" gasped Boddy. "Not —"

"Yes."

"Pitty-Pat!"

Tearfully, Mr. Boddy knelt down to examine the body of his beloved parrot.

"The window was closed, Mr. Boddy," Mrs. White stammered. "I guess poor Pitty-Pat flew into the window and . . . and now he's, he's —"

Mr. Boddy let out a sob and finished his maid's sentence. "Dead!"

One hour later . . .

One hour later, all of the guests gathered outside the mansion at the Boddy Family Cemetery.

Mr. Boddy stood before a tiny coffin, wringing a wet hanky with both hands.

"Dearest Pitty-Pat," Mr. Boddy began. "I am burying you alongside my own grave so that someday I may be with you . . . again."

"There, there," said plump Mrs. Peacock, gently patting her host. "Pitty-Pat's just flown to the great birdcage in the sky."

"No, no," cried Mr. Boddy. "Pitty-Pat's dead."

Mrs. Peacock looked blue. "Mr. Boddy! Don't say dead. It's a bad word. It's rude!"

Mr. Boddy sniffled.

"Now, now," said Colonel Mustard, slapping Boddy's back. "A gentleman must always be brave."

Mr. Boddy tried to be brave, but a loud sob escaped him. And another. He ran from the cemetery, weeping.

"Well, I guess the funeral's over," said Mr. Green coldly.

"Poor birdie," added Professor Plum.

Miss Scarlet batted her long dark lashes. She ran her dark red nails through the little bit of reddish hair on Plum's head. "Oh, now, don't pretend you liked Pitty-Pat. None of us did. Why, Mr. Green, you once tried to strangle that bird."

"It pecked my ear!" Mr. Green protested. His eyes narrowed to the size of poison darts. "And what are you suggesting, anyway? If you're implying anything, I'll beat you to a pulp."

"Threatening a woman?" cried Colonel Mustard. He slapped Green in the face with his glove. "I challenge you to a duel."

"A duel? In a cemetery?" Mrs. Peacock trembled with outrage. "Why, that's rude!"

Mustard turned yellow. "You're right," he said. "Sorry."

"It's true what you say, Miss Scarlet," mused Professor Plum. "I wasn't fond of the little creature. It pooped on my book."

"It stole my anchovies," added Colonel Mustard.

"It ate my red rouge," said Miss Scarlet bitterly. "I never let anyone touch my makeup."

"It tried to nest in my feather duster," said Mrs. White.

"And it called me a bad word," said Mrs. Peacock with a frown.

"Hmm. So none of us liked the bird," began the Colonel. He knelt down and examined the dead bird carefully. "Then we all had a motive for —"

"For?" prompted Mr. Green.

"For murder," finished the Colonel.

"Murder?" Mrs. Peacock looked faint.

"Yes, murder. Look at the wound. Someone could have hit Pitty-Pat on the head with a blunt instrument. Then the killer could have placed the parrot beneath the closed window to make it look like an accident."

"Poppycock," snarled Mr. Green. "Let's bury the thing."

"I've made inquiries," said the Colonel, ignoring him. "I know that at the time of the 'accident,' three of us had blunt weapons. Professor Plum had the Candlestick. You, Mr. Green, had the Wrench. And Miss Scarlet had the Lead Pipe."

"Nonsense," sputtered Mr. Green as he casually tossed the Wrench into the bushes.

"However," continued the Colonel, "only two of us were in the Conservatory at all today. And one of those two was not Miss Scarlet."

"Thank you for clearing my name," said Miss Scarlet, blushing bright red. She leaned over and planted a big loud kiss on the Colonel's cheek. Her lips left their mark in red lipstick.

"Yes. Well. Ahem. There's one final clue," stammered the Colonel. "At the time of Pitty-Pat's unfortunate demise, I was in the Billiard Room. I was playing snooker with Mr. Green and Professor Plum."

"You were?" said Professor Plum, looking surprised. "Oh, yes, quite right, so you were. It slipped my mind. Well, then, I think I know who killed the dirty birdy!"

WHO KILLED PITTY-PAT?

6

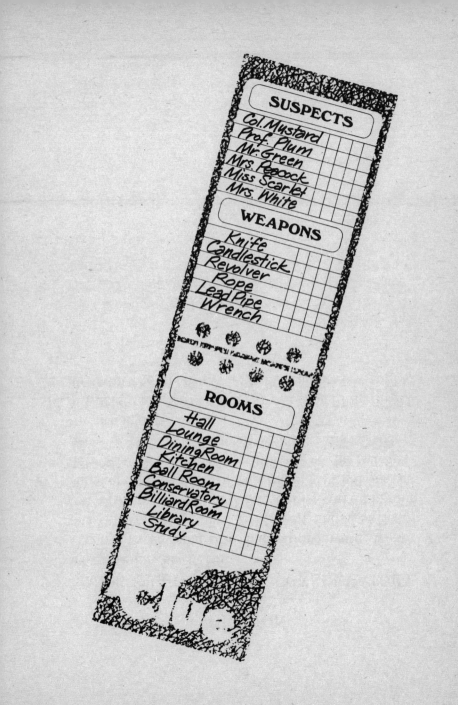

SOLUTION

MISS SCARLET in the CONSERVATORY with the LEAD PIPE

Only three suspects had appropriate weapons — Professor Plum, Mr. Green, and Miss Scarlet. Professor Plum and Mr. Green were playing snooker at the time of the murder. That leaves only Miss Scarlet. And, while one of the two suspects in the Conservatory was not Miss Scarlet, the other one was!

Luckily for Miss Scarlet, Professor Plum forgot all about the mystery, and she was never caught.

2.
Who Stole Miss Scarlet's Diamonds?

"AH, MR. BODDY!" EXCLAIMED MISS Scarlet as she swept into the Study. "Alone at last."

"Yes, yes," agreed her cheerful host, "except for me, of course."

Miss Scarlet looked confused.

"And except for . . ." Mr. Boddy gestured toward Mrs. White, who sat slumped in the dark leather armchair, snoring loudly.

Miss Scarlet drew closer. She draped her red boa over Mr. Boddy's shoulders. She lowered her voice to a silky whisper. "Reginald, darling. I've wanted a moment alone with you all evening."

Mr. Boddy blushed. "Oh, have you?"

"Yes, dearest. You see, I have these . . ."

She lowered her voice still further.

"Diamonds." She delicately fingered her large, glittering diamond necklace.

Mr. Boddy stared at the jewels and said, "Diamonds? What diamonds? Oh, those diamonds!"

Mrs. White let out a giant snore as she slept

peacefully in the armchair. Miss Scarlet eyed her for a moment, and then continued. "I was wondering if you had a place where I could keep them safe overnight?"

"Of course. Behind my ducks."

Miss Scarlet arched her pencil-thin, dark eyebrows.

"Ducks?"

"Yes, you know. Quack! Quack!" Mr. Boddy crossed to the Study wall and pointed to the painting that hung there. Three ducks flew over a large pond, quacking. He lifted the painting off the wall. Behind it was a large, gray metal safe.

"Ah," sighed Miss Scarlet. "Perfect!" She unclasped the necklace. Mr. Boddy turned to the safe. He put one hand on the dial. Then he turned back to look at Miss Scarlet. She was looking at him intensely.

"Er . . . Miss Scarlet. . . . This will sound silly. But the combination to the Boddy safe has been a secret in the Boddy family for generations. Would you mind . . . ?"

"Of course," Miss Scarlet said, and she sailed out of the room. "I'll be in the Library when you're done."

Mr. Boddy watched her go. Then he locked the door behind her. He left the latchkey in the keyhole, just in case anyone tried to peep in. Then he bent over and peered into Mrs. White's eyes.

They were tightly shut. She was still sound asleep.

"Good," he told himself, returning to the wall safe. "Now I have total privacy."

He was wrong.

For no sooner had he locked the Study door than Colonel Mustard had appeared by the door. He pressed his ear to the door to listen.

Then there was the secret door that led to the secret passageway to the Kitchen. The door was locked. But Professor Plum stood hidden behind it. He had overheard Mr. Boddy's entire conversation with Miss Scarlet.

And then there was the face pressed against the Study window. Mr. Green.

And of course Mrs. White wasn't really sleeping. As soon as Mr. Boddy turned his back, she opened her eyes slightly to form narrow slits. She watched as her employer silently turned the dial of the safe.

Hours later . . .

Hours later, a zigzag of lightning cracked down onto the mansion's vast green grounds. For an instant, the huge twelve-gabled house was lit up brightly. Thunder boomed. A driving rain slashed noisily downward.

Then utter darkness returned. But if someone

had been watching the mansion when the lightning struck, they would have caught a glimpse of a masked figure.

The masked figure stood by a third-floor window. The figure clutched the gold Candlestick in a black-gloved hand. The Candlestick held a lit, white candle, guiding the thief through the mansion's many dark, narrow passageways.

The masked figure moved stealthily down the carpeted stairs.

Just then, a squat balding man in green pajamas emerged from his bedroom. "Three sheep!" snarled the man. "Four sheep! And if I catch any of you sheep, I'll cook you for supper!"

It was Mr. Green, who couldn't sleep. He began climbing down the carpeted stairs.

The masked figure ducked into the shadows in the nick of time. Mr. Green passed by, only a few inches away. "Six sheep!" he growled. "Why can't I sleep! Seven sheep!"

The figure continued quietly downward. Down to the first floor, into the Kitchen, and through the secret passageway into the Study.

Using two gloved hands, the thief carefully removed the duck painting. Knowing the combination by heart, the masked figure easily opened the safe's massive door.

Inside lay the gleaming jewels.

The next morning . . .

"My diamonds! They're gone!"

Miss Scarlet swooned into the arms of Professor Plum.

"I'm so sorry," Mr. Boddy told her, wringing his hands. "I can't understand how anyone could have known the combination to my safe! Do you have any idea, Professor?"

"Let me see . . ." The Professor scratched his head with one hand. He gripped his book with the other. That left no hands to hold Miss Scarlet, who crashed to the Ball Room floor. "Sorry," he said. "I forgot I was holding you."

"You're all suspects," gasped Miss Scarlet as she got back to her feet. She pointed at the five other guests. "All of you."

"Including you," observed Mrs. Peacock dryly.

"Me!" Miss Scarlet's voice went up three octaves. "Why would I steal my own diamonds?"

"To collect one million dollars worth of insurance," said Mrs. Peacock. She held up an insurance form. "This fell out of your overnight bag. I've been meaning to give it back to you all weekend."

WHO STOLE MISS SCARLET'S DIAMONDS?

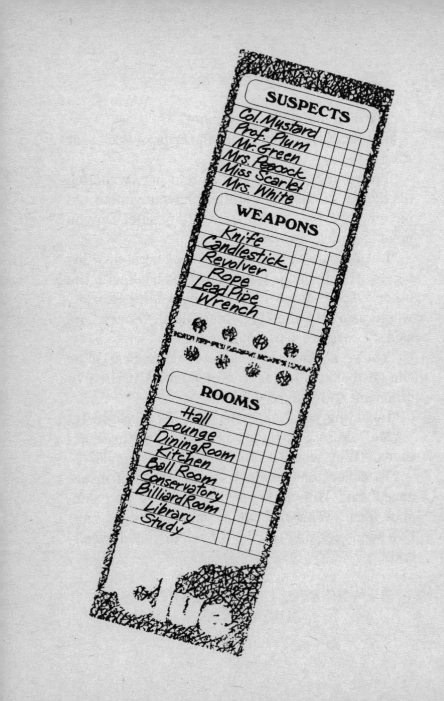

SOLUTION

MRS. WHITE in the **STUDY** with the **CANDLESTICK**

Only two suspects could have seen Mr. Boddy open the safe and, thus, could have memorized the combination: Mrs. White and Mr. Green. We can eliminate Mr. Green as a suspect. He was busy counting sheep on the stairway. That leaves Mrs. White. She was the masked figure with the Candlestick.

She's now a millionaire. But to avoid suspicion, she knows she must never sell — or even wear — the diamonds. Alas, she must keep on working as Mr. Boddy's bitter maid.

3.
Happy Birthday, Mr. Green

"**A**H," SIGHED MR. GREEN AS HE UN-wrapped Mrs. White's gift. "Just what I need. A Lead Pipe!"

"And may this present light up your life," said Mrs. Peacock.

"A gold Candlestick!" marvelled Mr. Green. "Stunning."

Colonel Mustard pulled his gift from behind his back. "I must tell you," he said, "my present cost a little more than I wanted to spend. But I decided to bite the bullet and —"

"A Revolver!" Mr. Green was delighted.

"This is from me," beamed Mr. Boddy. He handed over a lumpy package. "I bet it's *knot* what you think it is."

"Rope!" Mr. Green chuckled merrily. Then he saw Miss Scarlet coming toward him with a shiny box wrapped with a giant pink bow. Mr. Green turned green. "Oh, Miss Scarlet, you're too, too kind."

"Not *a' tool*," said Miss Scarlet with a wink.

"A Wrench!" Mr. Green was beside himself. "Gee, this is the best birthday I've ever had. My thanks to all of you."

Just then, the Dining Room door swung open. In walked Mrs. White, the maid. She carried a large green cake covered with burning green candles. She was smiling sweetly. Mr. Boddy flicked off the lights. In the secrecy of darkness, Mrs. White's expression changed to a bitter sneer.

The guests began to sing "Happy Birthday" to Mr. Green.

"Make a wish," Miss Scarlet cooed in Mr. Green's ear.

Mr. Green wished that Miss Scarlet would coo into his ear more often. Then he blew out his candles and the room plunged into total darkness.

"Hey! What's going on? Who turned out the lights?" cried a familiar voice. There was a crash. A yell. A scream.

When the lights were turned on, a chair lay overturned on the floor. Splattered beside it lay Mr. Green's green cake. Standing next to the mess, with cake on his hands, was a bewildered Professor Plum.

"What's going on here?" he demanded. "Someone turned the lights off just as I was coming in . . ."

"It's a birthday party," hissed Mr. Green. "And you just ruined my cake!"

17

"A birthday party!" Professor Plum slapped the side of his balding head, covering himself with green icing. "So that's where I was supposed to be tonight. I completely forgot!"

He put his arm around the furious Mr. Green, plastering Mr. Green's green suit with green icing. "Listen," he whispered, "help me out here, would you? Whose birthday is it?"

"It's mine, you donkey!"

"Donkey!" gasped Mrs. Peacock. "How rude!"

"Oh, yes, yes, yes, now I remember," said Plum. "A birthday party for Mr. Green. Yes."

"Ah, Professor — we've all given Mr. Green *our* gifts," Mr. Boddy said nervously. "Maybe now would be a good time for you to give him your present."

"My present?" Professor Plum frowned. He stared at his empty, icing-covered hands. He licked a finger. "Mmm, yes, my present is the Knife, now where did I leave it?"

"Oh, great!" snapped Mr. Green. "First you forget my party, then you forget my present. What's next?"

"I forget," said Plum. Then he made a funny face. "Uh-oh," he said.

"What?" barked Green.

"I just remembered something else."

Mr. Green waited. Finally, he yelled, "What?!"

"I got you two presents," Plum said.

Green's angry face turned into a smile. "Nothing wrong with that."

"And the second present is a time bomb that's going to go off in about . . ." Plum looked at his watch. "Oh, I'd say ninety seconds."

All the guests looked at one another blankly. Then, they all screamed in unison. "A TIME BOMB!"

"Why would anyone do anything so stupid?" asked Mustard.

"I thought it would liven up the party," Plum said. "Believe me, I didn't plan on things working out this way, I was going to turn the thing off right after you opened it. I mean, this way, the whole mansion is going to be blown to smithereens."

All the guests grabbed Plum. "Think! What room did you leave the bomb in?" they all asked at once.

"Please," said Plum. "Not all at once, it makes it too hard to understand what you're saying."

"But we're all saying the same thing," they all said at once. "Now what room did you leave it in?"

"I don't know," Professor Plum said, worriedly wiping green icing through his hair. "All I know is that I came in here empty-handed."

"Sixty seconds left," announced Mr. Boddy, looking at his watch.

"I'll check the Library," cried Mustard, rushing out.

"I'll check the Ball Room," called Mrs. White, and she ran out as well.

"Think back, Professor," urged Mrs. Peacock. "Try to retrace your steps."

"Retrace my steps? Okay, but why?" Professor Plum began walking backward.

"No, no, not like that!" cried Miss Scarlet.

"Look out!" shrieked Mrs. Peacock.

Plum was walking backward out the doorway. By sheer luck, he managed to miss Boddy's priceless Ming vase. But he knocked a picture off the wall. The picture crashed into the vase.

"Don't worry about that now," yelled Boddy. "There are only fifty seconds left."

They all raced to the Lounge.

"Now," called Mrs. Peacock as they ran, "where did you wrap the gift?"

"In the Billiard Room," answered the Professor.

"Forty seconds!" yelled Boddy from the rear.

"And what did you do next?" asked Mrs. White, when they were in the Lounge.

Professor Plum scratched his head. "I started thinking about my latest research project, the sleeping habits of snails. And I, um, went for a stroll."

"Thirty seconds!"

"And where did you go on this stroll of yours?" asked Miss Scarlet.

"Hmm. I remember I went into the Conservatory and then to the Lounge."

"And then?" prodded Mrs. Peacock.

"And then I went to the Library. And then to the Hall. Then to the Ball Room. And finally, to the party in the Dining Room."

"Twenty seconds!"

"Mr. Boddy," said Professor Plum. "I don't want to be rude. But what is this crazy obsession you've developed about time?"

"The bomb!" gasped Boddy. "The bomb!"

"Oh, yes," said Plum thoughtfully. Then they all started running again. They rushed into the Ball Room. Mrs. White was already there. "No bomb," she said. "I've gone through this room with a fine-toothed comb."

"Ten seconds!" called Boddy.

"Wait!" exclaimed the Professor. "I remember having the gift in the Library."

"I already searched the Library," Colonel Mustard shouted as he rushed into the room. "It's not there."

"Five," said Boddy. "Four . . . three . . ."

Professor Plum sat down at the grand piano. "If only I could remember," he said, clutching his head with both hands.

"Wait!" cried Mrs. Peacock. "I've just figured

out where the Professor left the Knife and the bomb!"

WHERE ARE THE KNIFE AND THE BOMB? IN THE BILLIARD ROOM, THE CONSERVATORY, THE LOUNGE, THE LIBRARY, THE HALL, THE BALL ROOM, OR THE DINING ROOM?

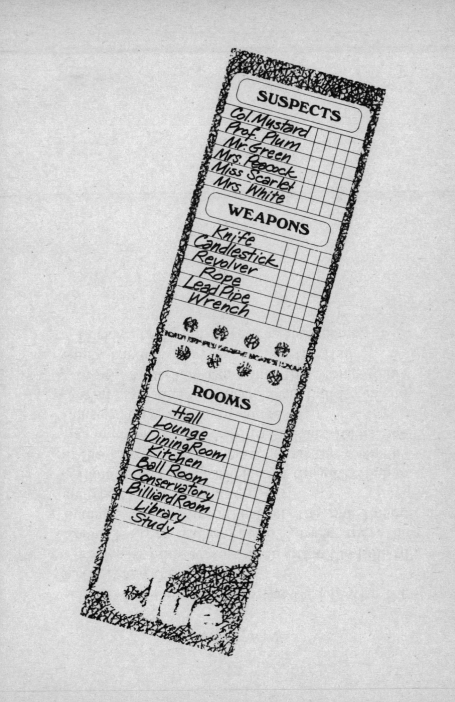

SOLUTION

PROFESSOR PLUM in the **HALL** with the **KNIFE** and the bomb

Professor Plum wrapped the gift in the Billiard Room. He then walked to the Conservatory, the Lounge, the Library, the Hall, the Ball Room, and the Dining Room.

Plum remembered still having the gift *with him* in the Library. So we can rule out the rooms he was in *before* the Library: the Billiard Room, the Conservatory, and the Lounge.

White and Mustard checked the Ball Room and Library. And Plum came into the Dining Room empty-handed. That leaves only the Hall. Luckily, he forgot to set the time bomb.

4.
The Ghost of Mrs. Boddy

"CONCENTRATE, EVERYONE!" COM-
manded Mrs. Peacock sternly. "Concentrate!"

The guests had gathered in the Dining Room.
The lights were turned off, the curtains closed.
Long black candles in elegant candlesticks flick-
ered from every surface. Incense perfumed the
air.

It was midnight on Saturday. Mr. Boddy had
asked his best friends to join him in tonight's séance.

"I must say, I don't really believe in this kind
of hocus-pocus," said Professor Plum.

"Hush!" said Mrs. Peacock. She adjusted her
blue turban. "You'll ruin the mood. Now, everyone hold hands."

Miss Scarlet firmly grasped one of Professor
Plum's hands. Mrs. White took his other hand.

"Well, this part is fun, anyway," he joked.

"Quiet!" barked Mr. Green. "Do you want to
ruin the séance?" Mr. Green was holding Colonel
Mustard's hand. He squeezed Mustard's hand so
hard that the Colonel challenged him to a duel.

"Gently, Gerald," Mrs. Peacock instructed Mr. Green. Green and Mustard resumed holding hands. Mrs. Peacock was holding the Colonel's other hand.

"Dear Bessie," intoned Mrs. Peacock. "Dear Bessie Boddy. Hear our plea. Your dear husband, Reginald Boddy, misses you terribly. He has gathered us here so that he can have a word with you. Are you there, Bessie?"

The group waited silently. They stared at the table, waiting for a signal. None came.

"My foot itches," said Professor Plum.

"Ssshhh!" said the rest of the group in unison.

Plum let go of Miss Scarlet's hand. He took the Knife, which lay hidden on his lap, and used it to scratch his foot inside his shoe. Then he took Miss Scarlet's hand again.

"Perhaps it would help," said Mrs. Peacock, "if you spoke to her directly, Reginald."

"All right," agreed Mr. Boddy. Mr. Boddy was holding hands with Miss Scarlet and Mr. Green. He cleared his throat. "Bessie," he said. "It's me, Reg. I miss you, Bessie. Bessie, are you okay?"

Suddenly, there was a sharp rapping sound from under the table. Everyone let out a gasp.

"One rap for yes, two raps for no, right, Bessie?" asked Mrs. Peacock.

Another sharp rap.

"That means yes," said Mrs. Peacock proudly.

"It's Bessie!" cried Mr. Boddy.

"Bessie," said Mrs. Peacock. "Do you mind if Reginald asks you a few questions?"

Two sharp raps.

"No, she doesn't mind," explained Mrs. Peacock. "Go ahead Reginald."

"Bessie," he said timidly, "are you all right?"

A loud, sharp rap.

"What a relief," sighed Mr. Boddy. "What a tremendous relief."

"Bessie?" Mrs. White asked timidly. "Are you happy in the great beyond?"

There was a loud sharp rap. Mr. Boddy sighed happily.

"Bessie?" barked Mr. Green. "Will you wait faithfully for Mr. Boddy until the day he joins you?"

"Mr. Green!" scoffed Mrs. Peacock. "What a rude question!"

But she was silenced by another sharp rap. The whole table shook from the force of it. "As you can see," said Mrs. Peacock, "the answer is a very loud *yes*."

Mr. Boddy stood up. There were tears in his eyes. "All of you have made me so happy," he told his guests. "Tonight will be the first night I sleep soundly since . . . since . . ."

He cleared his throat. "Good-bye for now, Bessie," he called.

The table rapped violently, shaking all over. It was Bessie saying good-bye.

Mr. Boddy thanked everyone again and again. Then he went upstairs to go to sleep.

"Well, he went to bed happy, didn't he?" Professor Plum said. "Even if it was all a fake."

"A fake?" said Miss Scarlet. "What are you talking about?"

"Well," Plum said. "Let's start by putting our cards on the table. I mean, our weapons."

"Weapons? What weapons?" said Mr. Green innocently.

"The weapons everyone has hidden on their laps," said Plum. He put the Knife on the table. "Now you, Mr. Green," he said.

Sheepishly, Mr. Green put the Lead Pipe on the table. It dropped with a sharp rap. The rest of the guests followed suit. Colonel Mustard had the Wrench. Miss Scarlet had the Revolver. Mrs. White had the Candlestick. And Mrs. Peacock had the Rope.

"All right," Mr. Green said, eyeing the others meanly. "Who was the wise guy who faked this business?"

"Whoever it was," said Mrs. Peacock, "it was someone who had a free hand during the séance. . . . Now, who wasn't holding hands?"

CAN YOU NAME THE FAKER?

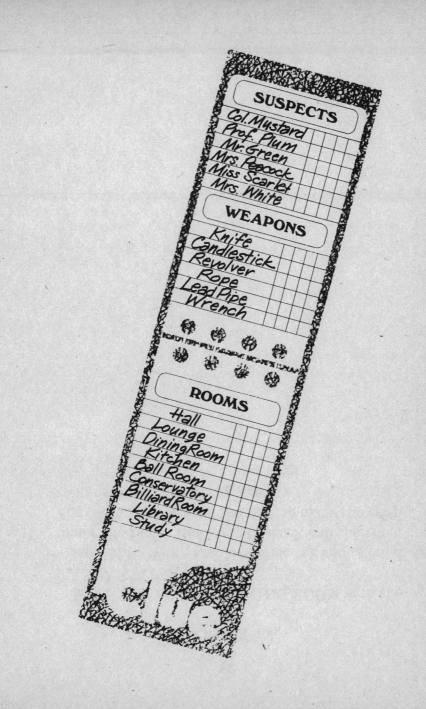

SOLUTION

MRS. WHITE in the DINING ROOM with the
CANDLESTICK

Only Mrs. White and Mrs. Peacock kept a hand
under the table. But Mrs. Peacock had the rope.
She couldn't have used the rope to make the crisp
rapping noises the group heard.

5.
Hide and Seek

"GOTCHA!" CRIED MR. GREEN.

He slapped Colonel Mustard on the back. Hard. Then he turned and ran back to home base, the Kitchen sink.

It was Friday night. Mr. Boddy had invited his six best friends to his mansion for a game of hide-and-seek. Mr. Green was "It."

"You're a home-base sticker," said Colonel Mustard as he followed Green into the Kitchen. "That's poor sportsmanship."

"I am not," said Green. "Just watch!" He tiptoed out of the Kitchen to search for the other hidden guests.

Suddenly there was a rush of footsteps. Plump Mrs. Peacock ran toward the Kitchen door. "Home free!" she cried as she raced toward the sink.

Unfortunately, Mrs. White had waxed the black-and-white tile floor earlier that morning. Mrs. Peacock slipped, and slid head first into the open Kitchen cabinets.

Mr. Green came back into the Kitchen and saw

her. "What a silly hiding place," he said to her backside. "Besides, no one is allowed to hide in the Kitchen." He tagged her. Then he ran off to look for more guests.

It took Mr. Green twenty minutes to find Miss Scarlet. She was hiding in the Hedge Maze on the back lawn. It took him thirty minutes to find Mr. Boddy. He was hiding in the clothes dryer! Then he started looking for Professor Plum.

Meanwhile . . .

Mrs. White was getting terribly bored. She was all alone in her hiding spot in the mansion, waiting to be found. She passed the first hour by thinking of the mean things she would do to the guests if they ever worked for her, instead of the other way round.

Now, to pass even more time, she began to dust. She dusted everything in the room. She even dusted the heavy, gold Candlestick on the mantel.

Unfortunately, when she placed the Candlestick down, it was a little too close to the edge. And when she bent down to dust below the mantel, the Candlestick fell and clunked her right on the head.

"Ouch!" said Mrs. White.

Then she dropped to the floor like a sack of beans.

It took Green forty minutes to find the Professor. He was hiding in a broom closet and forgot to come out.

"Well, that's everyone," he told the rest of the guests in the kitchen. "Great game. I won!"

"Not yet you didn't," said Mr. Boddy. "You still have to find Mrs. White."

"Wow," said the Colonel. He checked his timepiece. "Has she got patience. She's stayed hidden for almost two hours now!"

"Oh dear," said Mr. Boddy. "I hope she's okay."

"Why wouldn't she be?" growled Green.

The guests marched from room to room and called, "Mrs. White! You can come out now. The game's over. Mrs. White?"

"I'll search the lawn," announced Colonel Mustard. He ran outside. He stood in the vast darkness of the back lawn. He couldn't see a thing. "It's as dark as the inside of my boot," he muttered.

He called for Mrs. White. He whistled. He howled. He yodelled. Not a sound. Then he took out his Revolver. He screwed on the special flare attachment. He aimed the Revolver straight up in the air. And fired.

Unfortunately, the Colonel's aim was a little off. The flare sailed straight through the Library window.

"Whoops," said the Colonel. "Fore!"

The flaming flare landed right between Mr. Boddy's dictionary and his encyclopedia of seashells. Both books caught on fire. Soon the whole Library was in flames.

"You know," said the Professor to the other guests, "I think Mrs. White must have gone back to the Kitchen."

"Why do you say that?" Mr. Boddy asked.

"Because I smell something burning."

"You're right," said Mr. Boddy. "Now that you mention it, it does smell like Mrs. White's pancakes. Done to a crisp, and then cooked for fifteen minutes more."

They looked in the Kitchen, but Mrs. White was not there.

"FIRE!" yelled Colonel Mustard, charging back into the house. "EVERYONE OUT!"

"But we can't leave now," said Mrs. Peacock, beginning to cough. "Mrs. White may still be hiding somewhere in the house."

"Right you are," said the Colonel, taking charge. "Everyone check a room. Then we'll meet outside."

"And hurry," urged Mr. Boddy. "Mrs. White's life is at stake!"

They all ran off in different directions.

A few minutes later, the guests had gathered again on the mansion's front lawn. Smoke and flames were pouring out of the mansion's open windows. Beads of sweat were popping out on everyone's red faces.

The Colonel lined up his troops and paced up and down in front of them. "Who checked what?" he demanded. "Sound off one at a time!"

"I checked the Library," said Mr. Green.

"I checked the Billiard Room and the Conservatory," said Miss Scarlet.

"I checked the Hall and the Lounge," said Mrs. Peacock.

"Uh, I checked either the Dining Room, the Study, or the Conservatory," said Professor Plum. "I can't remember which."

"Great," cried the Colonel, twisting his hands in frustration. "All right, everyone stay outside. I'll take care of this."

Gallantly, the Colonel charged back into the burning house. He checked the Dining Room. Mrs. White was not there, and the smoke grew so thick that even the brave Colonel was driven out of the mansion.

Meanwhile, Mrs. White still lay unconscious. The flames curled slowly toward the hem of her black and white dress. She had only seconds to live. . . .

As luck would have it, no two rooms were checked twice.

CAN YOU FIGURE OUT WHICH ROOM
MRS. WHITE IS IN, IN TIME TO SAVE
HER LIFE? IS IT THE LOUNGE, THE
DINING ROOM, THE KITCHEN, THE
HALL, THE BALL ROOM, THE STUDY,
THE LIBRARY, THE BILLIARD ROOM,
OR THE CONSERVATORY?

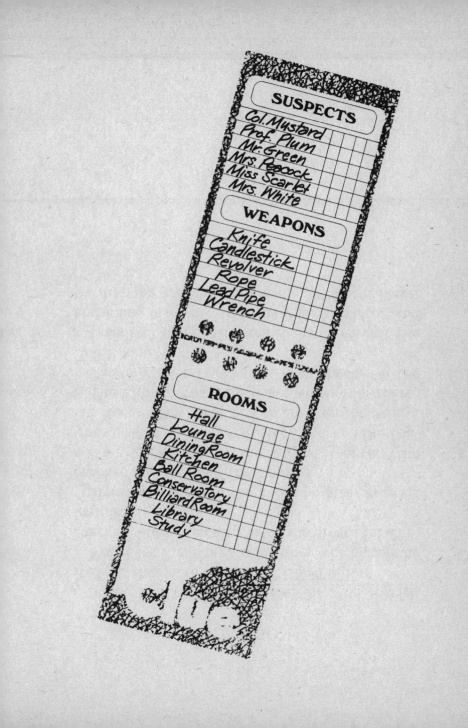

SOLUTION

MRS. WHITE unconscious in the BALL ROOM, thanks to the CANDLESTICK

Professor Plum can't remember which room he checked, but you can, by using the process of elimination.

Mr. Green checked the Library. Mrs. Peacock checked the Hall and the Lounge.

Miss Scarlet checked the Billiard Room and the Conservatory. Colonel Mustard checked the Dining Room. That means Plum checked the Study. The Kitchen was home base. No one was there. The only room that hadn't been checked is the Ball Room.

Luckily, Colonel Mustard rushed back into the house one last time. He saved Mrs. White. And the arriving fire engines quickly put out the blaze.

6.
Where There's Smoke, There's Fire!

IT WAS THE MIDDLE OF THE NIGHT. MR. Boddy's mansion was on fire again. Orange flames and black smoke poured out of the open windows. There were fire fighters everywhere. Fire fighters on the ground. Fire fighters manning hoses. Fire fighters on ladders. Fire fighters inside the burning house.

From the safety of the mansion grounds, three pajama-clad guests were watching the fire fighters as they wrestled the blaze.

"Some house-warming party," said Professor Plum.

"Yes," agreed Miss Scarlet. "It seems Mr. Boddy got the house a little too warm."

"It does seem a horrible shame," said Mrs. White. "He just got the place fixed up after the last fire. Then he has all his friends over for a party to celebrate. And wouldn't you know, the mansion is burning down all over again."

She looked sad. But that was because it was dark out. If Plum or Miss Scarlet had looked closer, they would have seen a wicked grin.

"You don't sound very sad about it," quipped Miss Scarlet. She wrapped her bright red bathrobe around her body more tightly.

"Oh, but I am," said Mrs. White sadly. "So very sad. First of all, I'm so sorry for Mr. Boddy. And don't forget. If this place burns down, I'm out of a job."

"I wonder how the fire got started this time," said Plum.

"Good question," agreed Miss Scarlet, eyeing him closely. "Where were you when Boddy's new fire alarm sounded?"

"I was in bed, lighting a candle," said Plum. Then he saw the suspicious look on Miss Scarlet's face. "Oh, but I put the candle out before I went to sleep." (STATEMENT #1)

"What about you?" Mrs. White asked.

"I started a fire in the Study fireplace," said Miss Scarlet. "But I promise you, I made sure that the fire was out before I went to bed." (STATEMENT #2)

"Looks like we all came close to starting a fire," said Mrs. White. "After I went to bed, I remembered that I left a pot of potatoes cooking on the Kitchen stove. But I went back downstairs and turned the stove off before the fire started." (STATEMENT #3)

"Mrs. White, your statement is a lie," Professor Plum accused. (STATEMENT #4)

40

"No, Professor, your first statement is a lie," answered Miss Scarlett. (STATEMENT #5)

The three guests were soon screaming at each other.

But the fact was, one of these three suspects had indeed started the fire.

And when you figure out who it was, you'll see that within their five statements, there was a total of three lies.

WHO STARTED THE FIRE?

Hint: To solve this mystery, you'll need to complete this chart. Mark all of the statements T for True or F for False.

Here are the statements again:

STATEMENT #1: "I put the candle out before I went to sleep," said Plum.

STATEMENT #2: "The fire was out before I went to bed," said Miss Scarlett.

STATEMENT #3: "I turned the stove off before the fire started," said Mrs. White.

STATEMENT #4: "Mrs. White, your statement is a lie," Professor Plum accused.

STATEMENT #5: "No, Professor, your first statement is a lie," said Miss Scarlet.

For example, let's say Professor Plum started the fire. Then his alibi, "I put the candle out before

41

I went to sleep," would be False. And his statement that Mrs. White is a liar would be False, as well. Why? Because if he started the fire, then her alibi is True.

SUSPECT	#1	#2	#3	#4	#5	NUMBER OF LIES
PLUM	F	T	T	F	T	2
SCARLET						
WHITE						

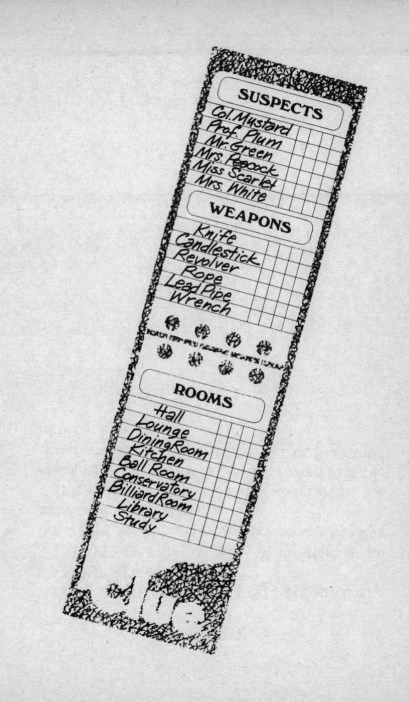

SOLUTION

MISS SCARLET in the **STUDY** with the **CANDLESTICK**

If Professor Plum or Mrs. White started the fire, there would be only two lies among the five numbered statements.

If it's Miss Scarlet, her alibi is a lie. So is the statement that Mrs. White is a liar. And so is the statement that Professor Plum is a liar. For a total of three lies.

7.
The Secret Changes Hands

"**T**HREE ROLLS OF FILM, AND NOTH-ing but bunny rabbits!" said Mr. Green with disgust. "Really, Mrs. Peacock, you ought to be ashamed of yourself."

"I'm sorry you don't like my photographs, Mr. Green," Mrs. Peacock answered stiffly. "I take pictures of what I like. And I like bunnies."

"Now, now," said Mr. Boddy. "Let's not argue. After all, each member of my photography club has his or her own taste."

"That's true," said Mr. Green. "I have good taste and she has bad taste."

"Good taste?" scoffed Mrs. Peacock. "Pictures of pro football?"

"That's right," barked Green. "Action shots!"

"But you photographed your TV set," laughed Mrs. Peacock. "I can't see a thing!"

"Well, even a fuzzy photo of a TV set is better than your pictures of bunnies!"

"I say," said Colonel Mustard, putting down his teacup. "I won't have you insulting the lady like this. I challenge you to a duel!"

Mr. Boddy jumped up. "Please! Please! No fighting!"

When the Colonel saw the pained look on Mr. Boddy's face, he tried to calm down.

"Listen," said Professor Plum. "We're all acting selfish. While we sit here and argue about our pictures, poor Mrs. White has to do all the work. Here, Mrs. White, let me help you clear these teacups."

"You're too kind," Mrs. White said sweetly. She waited until she had turned her back before she rolled her eyes.

"Now there's a true gentleman," said Mrs. Peacock.

"Let me help, too!" said Mr. Green, who didn't want to be left out.

"And there's a true ninny," Mrs. Peacock added.

Luckily, he didn't hear her.

Everyone helped Mrs. White clear the dishes from the Library and take them into the Kitchen.

But no one noticed . . . that one of the guests . . . had slipped away . . . through the secret passageway in the Kitchen . . . and into the Study.

Like all of the photography club members, this tall, thin man had a camera slung over his shoulder. He locked the door behind him. He walked over to the wooden cabinet. The bottom drawer, his employer had said. The documents would be in the bottom drawer. He pulled on the knob.

It was locked.

The man adjusted his eyeglasses nervously. He fiddled with his purple bow tie. Professor Plum was starting to sweat. He had never done anything like this before. Spying on Mr. Boddy! Normally he wouldn't consider such an assignment. But he needed the money for his new research project: trying to find out which animal in nature blinked most often on an average day. And the government had really put the lid on funding for blink research.

He yanked on the drawer with all his might. He wrestled with it, kicked it, he even bit it. Then he remembered that his employer had given him a key.

He used the key to open the drawer. There were the documents, neatly stacked in a pile. Mr. Boddy was a consultant for a local gumdrop company. These documents detailed Boddy's discovery: a way to make gumdrops that lasted in your mouth for hours! A rival gumdrop company had hired Plum to find out the secret.

Plum photographed Boddy's secret documents as fast as he could. He snapped a whole roll of film. He quickly removed the roll from the camera and slipped it into the right pocket of his purple cardigan sweater.

When he came back into the Library, there was a huge round of applause.

"Bravo!" cried Mr. Boddy.

"Well done!" shouted Colonel Mustard.

"Er . . . I'm not sure what you're referring to," mumbled Plum. "I apologize for wandering off like that. You know how forgetful I am. I mean, it's not as if I were spying on you, Mr. Boddy, or anything like that!"

Luckily, no one was listening. The Professor now realized who all the applause was for. Mr. Green was entertaining his fellow guests with amateur magic tricks.

Green was holding Miss Scarlet's red silk handkerchief. He waved his hand over it. It turned bright green!

Everyone cheered loudly. Professor Plum sat down in the one empty chair, right next to Green.

Mr. Green immediately leaned over and pulled an egg from behind the Professor's ear. Everyone laughed and applauded some more.

"You got any more eggs?" asked Green.

"Why, no, I —"

But Mr. Green pulled more eggs from the Professor's nose and mouth. "Holding out on me, eh?" Green teased.

"No, not at all, I —"

"So many eggs. You must have a chicken around here somewhere, to lay all these eggs."

"A chicken? Oh, absolutely not, I — "

But Mr. Green was patting him up and down, searching for a chicken. And now he was patting the right pocket of Plum's purple cardigan. Green felt the roll of film. The roll of spy film.

"Aha!" cried Green. "I've found it!"

The other guests leaned forward. "What is it?" "Let's see!" "Show us what he has in his pocket!"

"No! No!" ranted Plum, getting angry. "You can't see."

"Oooh," said Green. "Something secret, is it?"

"No, no, it's not secret at all," said Plum. "I just don't want —"

But it was too late.

Mr. Green had succeeded in squeezing his hand into Plum's sweater pocket.

He pulled out a chicken!

This won him another chorus of cheers. Plum wiped the sweat from his brow. This spying business just wasn't for him. Luckily, Green hadn't gotten suspicious about the roll of film after all. He just wanted to do his chicken trick. What a relief!

Plum carefully felt his pocket.

It was empty.

Mr. Green had stolen the roll of film. Now Plum's roll lay with Green's roll of film in Mr. Green's pocket.

Oh, dear, thought Plum.

"Marvelous tricks, old boy," Colonel Mustard was saying. He clapped Mr. Green on the back. "Marvelous."

However, he wasn't just patting Mr. Green to be nice. He had seen Mr. Green steal the Professor's roll of film and had figured out it must be valuable. So now, he slipped his hand into Mr. Green's pocket and stole one of the two rolls. He added the roll to his own roll of film already in his pocket.

Oh, dear, thought Plum, Mustard's got my film. He stood up and began slapping his pockets. "Matches," he said absently to himself.

Mr. Green was now doing knot tricks with the Rope. Plum stood beside the Colonel. "I've forgotten my matches," he mumbled, "as usual." Then he slapped the Colonel's pockets.

"I beg your pardon," said Mustard.

"Sorry, sorry," Plum said, "just looking for matches."

The Colonel lent him his silver lighter.

"Thank you, thank you," said Plum. He moved back to his seat. To be safe, he had taken both rolls of film from Mustard's pocket.

But Mustard wasn't the only one who had seen Mr. Green steal the film. So had Mrs. White. "Let me get that plate out of your way," she now told Mr. Green, leaning over him. She removed the half-empty plate of chocolate chip cookies from the table. She also removed the other roll of film from Mr. Green's pocket.

PLUM'S ORIGINAL ROLL OF FILM HAS NOW CHANGED HANDS EXACTLY TWICE. DOES PLUM HAVE HIS OWN ROLL OF FILM BACK? AND IF HE DOESN'T HAVE HIS FILM, WHO DOES?

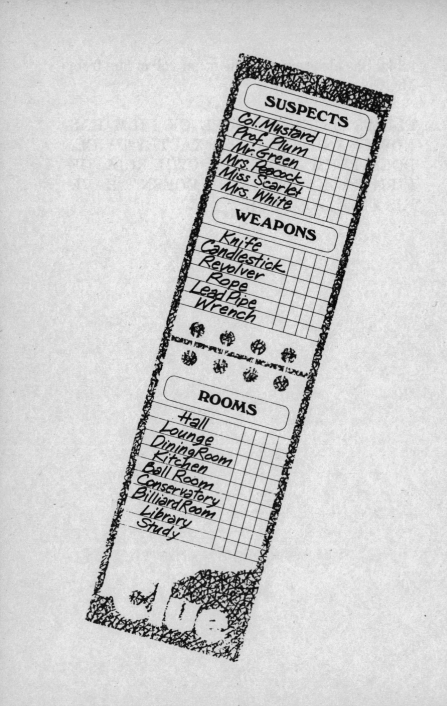

SOLUTION

MRS. WHITE in the LIBRARY with PLUM's film

If Plum had his own roll of film back, it would mean that the film had changed hands three times. First to Green, then to the Colonel, then back to Plum. If Mrs. White has the film, and she does, it's changed hands only twice. First to Green, then to White.

Luckily for Plum, he is able to steal the roll back from Mrs. White. He destroys the film and vows never to spy again.

8.
The Sleepwalking Killer

"**M**MMMMM . . . HUNGRY . . . mmmmmmm . . ."

The sleepwalker kept mumbling.

"Food . . . food . . . Kitchen . . . Kitchen . . ."

The sleepwalker's arms were stretched out straight like the arms of Frankenstein's monster. The sleepwalker tottered through room after room of Mr. Boddy's mansion.

It was three in the morning. The sleepwalker was one of Mr. Boddy's weekend guests. The only sounds in the house were the ticking of clocks and the loud snores of the other guests. And, the sound of the sleepwalker mumbling, "Food . . . food . . ."

In the Kitchen, the sleepwalker stumbled to the fridge. The sleepwalker took out a package of blue cheese and sniffed it.

"Gross . . . gross . . ." said the sleepwalker, gagging.

Then the sleepwalker took a bite of Mrs. White's peach pie.

"Yum . . . yum . . ."

And smeared some blueberry jam on a piece of cold toast.

"Tasty . . . tasty . . ."

And washed it all down with a swig of chocolate milk.

"Ahhhhh . . ."

Still sleeping soundly, the sleepwalker now marched straight out of the Kitchen.

Except, the sleepwalker took the wrong door and was now in the secret passageway.

"Narrow . . . narrow . . . dark . . . dark . . ."

The passageway led to the Study. Sitting on the mantel over the fireplace was the Revolver.

The sleepwalker picked up the Revolver. A puzzled look came over the sleepwalker's face.

"Gun? . . . Gun?"

The puzzled look went away. Now the sleepwalker was nodding.

"Yes . . . yes. . . . Kill . . . kill . . ."

Barefoot, the sleepwalker marched out of the Study and into the Hall.

"Kill . . . kill . . ."

Out of the Hall and into the Lounge.

"Kill . . . kill . . ."

Through the secret passageway and into the Conservatory.

"Kill . . . kill . . ."

And then into the Ball Room.

Where poor Miss Scarlet had fallen asleep on the red sofa.

The sleepwalker aimed the Revolver at Miss Scarlet's heart.

"Kill . . ." said the sleepwalker.

The sound of the sleepwalker's voice awakened Miss Scarlet. She looked at the sleepwalker, saw the Revolver, and screamed.

Which was when the sleepwalker fired. Miss Scarlet's scream died away quickly. The sleepwalker dropped the Revolver and walked out of the room.

Still sleeping.

Still mumbling.

"Bed . . . bed . . . tired . . . tired . . . sleep."

Minutes later . . .

Mr. Boddy's guests were sound sleepers. Miss Scarlet's scream and the sound of the Revolver woke up only one guest: Mr. Green.

Mr. Green had a loud voice. He bellowed so loudly that he woke up the others in no time at all.

The guests helped Mr. Boddy search the house. Their faces reddened with horror when they found Miss Scarlet lying in a pool of red blood on the red sofa.

But they had no idea who had done the terrible deed.

It seemed that everyone except Mr. Boddy had raided the fridge that night.

Only Mr. Green, Mrs. White, Professor Plum, and Mrs. Peacock had peach pie crumbs on their pajamas and nightgowns.

And only the palms of Colonel Mustard, Mrs. Peacock, and Mrs. White were sticky with blueberry jam.

And only Mr. Green, Professor Plum, and Mrs. White had chocolate mustaches.

Of course, only the sleepwalker had the telltale evidence of all three snacks — peach pie, blueberry jam, and chocolate milk.

WHO WAS THE SLEEPWALKING KILLER?

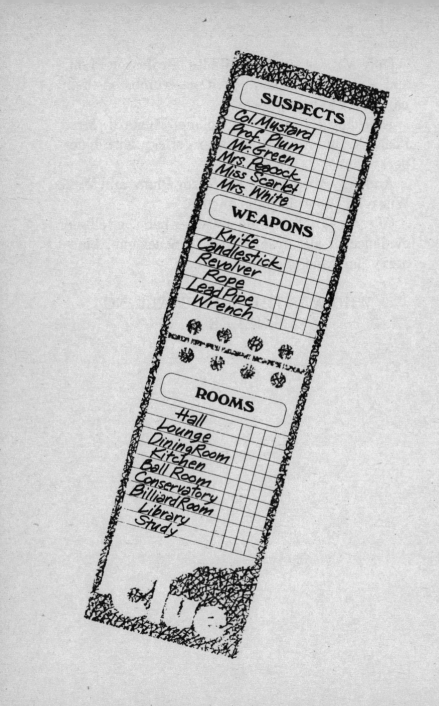

SOLUTION

MRS. WHITE with the REVOLVER in the BALL ROOM

The culprit must have all three clues. A lack of peach pie crumbs, therefore, rules out Mustard. And a lack of blueberry jam rules out everybody except Mrs. Peacock and Mrs. White. But Mrs. Peacock doesn't have a chocolate mustache.

In the future, Mr. Boddy promises to lock Mrs. White in her room.

Luckily, Miss Scarlet was not hurt. She had moved out of the way just in time. When the shot came, she fainted. The bullet struck a glass of red passion fruit juice she had left on the arm of the sofa, and it had spilled, looking like blood.

9.
Miss Feather's Gossip Column

"**A** GENTLEMAN TO SEE YOU, SIR," Mrs. White said. She curtsied and smiled sweetly.

"Show him in," Mr. Boddy told his maid. He looked back at the tax form he was studying. "Good," he muttered. "This year I only owe ten million dollars."

Behind his back, Mrs. White was thumbing her nose at him and sticking out her tongue. He turned and looked at her. She smiled. "I was just going," she said sweetly.

Then she showed in the visitor.

The visitor turned out to be the editor in chief of the town's paper. "I'm sorry to disturb you, Reginald," the editor said. "But I wanted to show you a column we're going to run in tomorrow's paper. I thought I owed you that courtesy."

He handed Mr. Boddy a sheet of paper. Mr. Boddy studied it for a moment. Then he let out a long, shuddering gasp. "No!"

That night . . .

That night, Mr. Boddy held an emergency meeting. Mr. Green, Miss Scarlet, Colonel Mustard, Mrs. Peacock, and Professor Plum all rushed to the mansion.

"What's the meaning of this?" Mr. Green demanded of Mrs. White. They were all in the Library waiting for Mr. Boddy.

"I have no idea, sir," Mrs. White said sweetly. She pretended to sneeze. Behind her hands she stuck out her tongue.

Just then, the door opened. It was Mr. Boddy. He looked very worried.

Everyone jumped up. Even Mrs. White.

"Sit, sit," said their host.

They all sat.

"Now," said Mr. Boddy. "I suppose you're all wondering why I've called you here tonight." He held up a piece of paper. "This is an advance copy of a column that will appear in tomorrow's *Little Falls Gazette*. The editor of the paper was kind enough to give it to me. Allow me to read it to you."

Mr. Boddy put on his bifocals and stared at the page. He cleared his throat several times. Then he read: " 'Big Doings in Little Falls,' a new column by Miss Feathers." He gazed around the room. "Any of you know a Miss Feathers, by any chance?"

As his gaze swept around the room, the guests lowered their eyes.

Mr. Boddy read on. " 'Last weekend I attended a dinner party thrown by Mr. Reginald Boddy, the richest man in Little Falls. While I was there, I had the opportunity to observe the other guests quite closely. I'm sorry to say they were a very rude bunch indeed.' "

Mr. Boddy's audience grumbled in disbelief.

"It gets worse," he said. He read, " 'Never in my life have I seen so many people with such bad manners gathered in one place. For instance, Mr. Gerald Green chews his food with his mouth open.' "

All around the room, mouths fell open in horror.

"That's a lie!" barked Green.

" 'As for Mr. Boddy, he may be filthy rich, but he has no class. Why, he never even puts his napkin on his lap.' "

"This is an outrage," murmured Miss Scarlet. "Why —"

" 'And then there is the shocking case of Miss Charlotte Scarlet.' "

"Uh-oh," said Miss Scarlet.

" 'Miss Scarlet wears dresses with bare shoulders! She is a shameless flirt. Why, Miss Scarlet likes to take tastes from men's plates! She throws herself at men.' "

"That's such a lie," said Miss Scarlet as she swooned into Professor Plum's arms.

" 'And then there's the case of Colonel Martin Mustard,' " read Boddy. " 'Colonel Mustard has the incredibly bad taste to fire off his Revolver during meals.' "

"I challenge whoever wrote this to a duel!" yelled Mustard. He fired off his Revolver. He nicked Plum's purple bow tie, spinning it round in a circle.

" 'Mrs. Wilhelmina White is Mr. Boddy's maid. She pretends to be sweet. But the truth is, I have never met a ruder person. She is always sticking out her tongue and thumbing her nose behind people's backs.' "

Mrs. White smiled sweetly. Then she stuck out her tongue.

Mr. Boddy read on. " 'Professor Paul Plum, a regular at Boddy's mansion, is a very forgetful man. This I can forgive. But I cannot forgive a man who forgets to use his napkin. I had to sit across from him for an hour, staring at a face smeared with cottage cheese.' "

"I knew I was forgetting something," said Professor Plum. He quickly removed his pocket hanky and wiped away the lump of cottage cheese that was still on his cheek.

"The article ends," said Boddy, "with a promise of more shocking gossip next week."

Gravely, Mr. Boddy folded the paper and put

it back in his pocket. "Now," he said, "I have reason to believe that one of us . . . one of the people in this very room . . . is Miss Feathers."

"That's nonsense," said Mrs. Peacock. "What makes you say a silly thing like that?"

"No," said Mr. Green. "Boddy's right. Who else could have known all that stuff about us?"

"Exactly," said Boddy.

"But who?" said Plum.

"Maybe it was you, Professor," said Mrs. White. "But you just forgot."

"Or you?" said Miss Scarlet, eyeing the maid.

"If you'll notice," said Mr. Boddy, "there is one person in this room who was not singled out for gossip."

Everyone's eyes darted back and forth as the guests tried to figure out who he meant.

"Ow!" said Plum. "My eyes hurt from all this darting back and forth. Just tell us who you mean."

Mr. Boddy paused. He looked down. Then he said it. "Mrs. Peacock."

Mrs. Peacock turned all the colors of the peacock feather in her blue hat.

"That's silly," she said. "I would never tell tales. Not in a million years."

"So you deny it?" growled Green.

"Absolutely!"

The group formed a small circle around her. They moved closer. Closer.

"You're making a mistake," said Mrs. Peacock. "I had nothing to do with that column."

Colonel Mustard cocked his Revolver.

"You know me better than that," said Mrs. Peacock. "I would never try to get any of you in trouble."

Mr. Green began patting his open palm with the Wrench.

"Unless of course . . ." she said, "unless of course you deserved it."

"Then it *was* you," said Miss Scarlet.

"Yes," Mrs. Peacock said defiantly. She held her head up high. "I am Miss Feathers! I'm not afraid of any of you!"

"Now Mrs. Peacock," said Mr. Boddy, "nobody wants to hurt you. The editor of the paper promised me that he won't run the story. All you have to do is call him and tell him."

Mr. Green hissed, "Will you tell him not to run this . . . this tommyrot!"

Mrs. Peacock shook violently. The peacock feather in her cap waved all around. "Mr. Green! I've warned you in the past about using bad words."

She pushed her way through the circle. "I had to write this column," she told them. "Because I was so shocked by all of your bad manners. Instead of trying to convince me to stop writing the column, you should worry about behaving properly and with good manners!"

Miss Scarlet removed the Lead Pipe from her red purse. "I take it you still mean to publish your column?"

"Yes!"

Professor Plum pulled a gold-handled Knife from its green sheath. "And there's nothing we can do to . . . er . . . convince you to change your mind?"

"Nothing!"

"Nothing at all?" asked Mrs. White, winding a long loop of Rope around her arm.

"I won't change a word!" insisted Mrs. Peacock. And with that she practically flew from the room.

Much later that night . . .

A group of masked figures gathered in Mr. Green's room. In the center of the room was a pile of weapons: a Knife, a Wrench, a Revolver, a Lead Pipe, and a Candlestick.

"All right," said Mr. Green, "let's get started. Mrs. White?"

"Yes, sir?" she said sweetly. But behind her mask she was making a face.

"You take the Revolver."

"Oh, but I don't know how to use it," she said, handing it back.

"Fine," he said, "I'll give you a different weapon." He handed her another one. When he had handed out all of the weapons, he said, "Okay, let's get to work. And when we're done, there will be no more Miss Feathers!"

The five masked figures tiptoed down the hall toward Mrs. Peacock's guest room.

"Wait," said Mr. Green. He stopped short just outside Mrs. Peacock's room. The four other masked figures all bumped into his back.

"You bumbling idiots!" hissed Green. "Now listen. Remember to keep your masks on, just in case anything goes wrong. Okay. Let's go!"

Green lowered his shoulder and ran at the closed door. But just before his shoulder hit the door, the door flew open.

All five attackers fell screaming into the dark room. They crashed against the wall. Then the door closed and locked.

"Good evening," said Mrs. Peacock. "How nice of you all to drop in."

One of the masked figures was back on his feet. He was waving a Lead Pipe.

"That's the trick, Mr. Green," yelled the attacker with the Candlestick. "Get her!"

The attacker with the Lead Pipe charged at Mrs. Peacock.

Luckily for Mrs. Peacock, as a young girl she had studied judo. She caught the attacker neatly and flipped him through the air. He crashed into the other wall.

Then a shot rang out. Mrs. Peacock ducked. "Ow!" said another one of the attackers.

Now two attackers rushed at her from either side. Mrs. Peacock ducked. The attackers crashed into each other and fell to the floor.

"Where did she go?" mumbled one of the confused attackers, waving her arms.

"I don't see her, Miss Scarlet . . ." said another.

"Where's the light switch, anyway?" asked a third.

These three attackers were holding the Wrench, the Revolver, and the Candlestick.

In the dark room, Mrs. Peacock couldn't be sure which one of the three masked figures was Miss Scarlet. Okay, Mrs. Peacock thought. So Miss Scarlet either has the Wrench, the Revolver, or the Candlestick.

As she thought about this, Mrs. Peacock snuck up behind all three attackers.

As a small girl, Mrs. Peacock had also taken karate. She gave a karate chop to each attacker and they fell to the floor.

Moments later, all five attackers were on their feet again. They had Mrs. Peacock by the throat.

Except that Mrs. Peacock had slipped away.

What they really had was each other by the throats.

Unable to breathe, the whole group fell to the floor again, gasping.

For a moment, the only sounds in the room were

gasping and chuckling. Mrs. Peacock was doing the chuckling. The sound of her laughing seemed to revive the attackers. They moaned one huge growl as they all got to their feet again.

"Laughing at me, eh? I challenge you to a duel!" cried one of the masked figures.

It was Colonel Mustard. But which one was he? Mrs. Peacock couldn't tell for sure, because two attackers were charging forward at the same time. So Mustard was either the one holding the Knife, or the one with the Candlestick. Luckily, as a small girl Mrs. Peacock had also taken a class in acrobatics. At the last second, Mrs. Peacock jumped. She grabbed onto the overhead light. She pulled herself up in the air and out of the way. And her attackers ran screaming into the wall.

"Here I am," said Mrs. Peacock from the center of the room.

All five attackers raced toward her at once.

Luckily, as a small girl Mrs. Peacock had also taken a class in ventriloquism. She had thrown her voice to the center of the room. She was actually hiding under the bed.

The attackers all crashed into one another head-first and fell in a perfect circle, out cold.

Mrs. Peacock crawled out from hiding and flicked on the lights.

"Now," she said to herself. "Which one of you is which?"

She bent over the first attacker. The unconscious figure was clutching the Knife. She pulled up the mask.

"Professor Plum," said Mrs. Peacock. "Tsk, Tsk. What a bad boy you are!"

She didn't have to lift any more of the masks. She now knew the identity of each attacker.

CAN YOU FIGURE OUT WHICH GUESTS HAD WHICH WEAPONS?

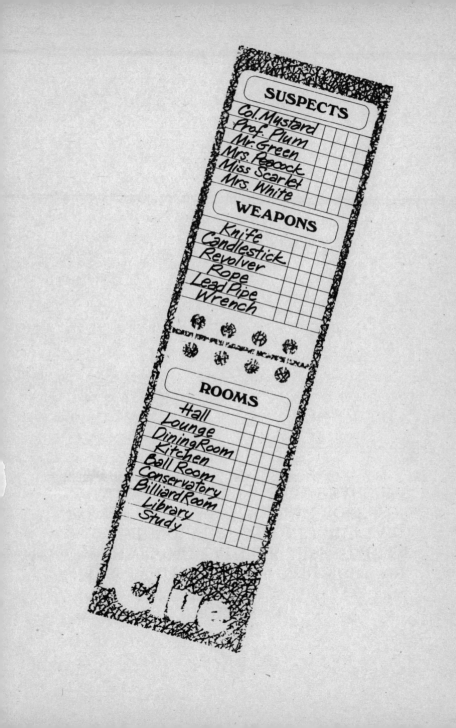

SOLUTION

MRS. WHITE with the WRENCH, MR. GREEN with the LEAD PIPE, MISS SCARLET with the REVOLVER, COLONEL MUSTARD with the CANDLESTICK, and PROFESSOR PLUM with the KNIFE in MRS. PEACOCK'S room!

10.
Who Was Fiddling Around?

"DEE - DAH - DEE - DAH - DEEDLE - DEE-dle-dee!!!"

Mr. Boddy was sawing away at his violin. And singing along. He played with such gusto that he finished three pages ahead of the other musicians.

"I win," he said with a happy grin.

It was Sunday. Mr. Boddy had invited his favorite friends over to play chamber music with him in the Ball Room.

There was one new face: a hunchbacked old woman who was playing second violin.

"Well," Mr. Boddy said as the concert drew to a close. "You certainly play a mean second fiddle."

"Why, thank you," said the old woman in a strange, high-pitched voice. "That's awfully sweet of you, I'm sure."

Funny, thought Mr. Boddy as the musicians packed up their instruments. I don't remember inviting her.

To the group he said, "I hope you'll all join me in the Dining Room. Mrs. White will be serving tea and her famous crumpets once she puts away her instrument."

"How delightful," squeaked the old woman.

"Yes," said Mr. Boddy. "By the way . . ." he began.

But the old woman said, "Excuse me a moment, will you? I have to go freshen up."

And she left the room.

When the guests gathered in the Dining Room, the old woman was no longer among them.

Even stranger! thought Boddy.

He was still carrying his violin case. He was going to lock it up in the family safe. It was a Stradivarius, after all. Worth a million dollars.

Then Boddy realized something else very strange.

The case in his hands felt awfully light.

He opened it up.

"Oh, no!" he cried. "My Stradivarius! It's been stolen! That woman!"

"Look!" cried Mrs. White. "There she goes!"

Mrs. White pointed out the Dining Room window. There was the hunchbacked old woman. She was galloping across the back lawn. Tucked under her arm was Mr. Boddy's violin!

The chase was on.

Mr. Boddy and the other guests chased the old woman through the hedge maze. But they all got bushed.

Then they chased her through the family cemetery. This must be a plot! thought Boddy.

Then they chased her through the miniature golf course, where Boddy's shoes began to hurt his feet. There must be a hole in one, he thought.

Suddenly he had another thought. He turned and ran back into the house.

In the Lounge, he found his invitation list for today's party. Gasping for breath, he tried to study the list.

NOTES ON WHOM I SHOULD INVITE TO MY MUSIC PARTY

First Violin — Me.
Second Violin — Whom should I invite?
First Viola — Any of the three women.
Second Viola — Any of the three women.
First Cello — Any of the three women.
Second Cello — Miss Scarlet or Professor Plum.
Piano — Not Professor Plum or Colonel Mustard.

Mr. Boddy scratched his head. He thought and thought. Sure enough, one of his regular music partners was missing from his list.

Meanwhile, the other guests had cornered the old woman by the badminton net.

"Give us back Mr. Boddy's fiddle, you old crone," snarled Mr. Green.

75

"Crone? Why, you cad!" The old woman seemed irate. She ripped off her mask. It wasn't an old woman at all. It was . . .

WHO WAS IT?

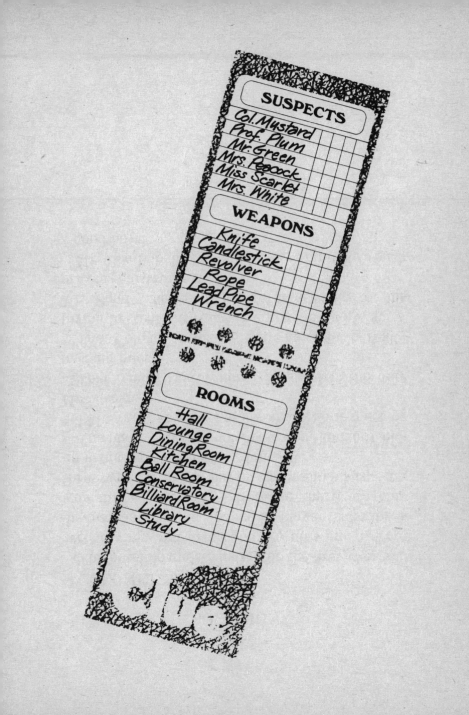

COLONEL MUSTARD

The possible guests listed for the first viola and second viola and first cello are all women. That means that the second cello player can't be a woman as well. Why? Because there are only three women on the list of six possible suspects. So it must be Professor Plum.

The piano player is not Professor Plum or Colonel Mustard. It can't be a woman. So it must be Mr. Green.

That means that Colonel Mustard is the only missing guest.

The Colonel explains that he wasn't really trying to steal the violin. He just wanted to show Mr. Boddy the need for better security for his priceless instrument.

Mr. Boddy believed and forgave him. He's such a good host!

11.
The Night the Maid Became a Zombie

A WATCH DANGLED IN FRONT OF MRS. White's face.

"Watch the watch," said the voice of the guest who stood before her. "Watch the watch."

The watch swung back and forth, back and forth.

"You will begin to feel sleepy," intoned the guest.

"Sleepy," repeated Mrs. White softly. Her face had become a blank mask.

"And your whole body will begin to feel light as a feather."

"Light as a feather . . ."

"Yes." The hypnotist glanced toward the Kitchen door. But no other guests were in earshot.

It was Friday night. Mr. Boddy had invited his favorite weekend guests to admire his latest art purchase. It was a tiny ancient Persian statuette made of pure gold. It was worth more than two million dollars!

"Now," the hypnotist told the maid, "I'm going to count backward from three. When I get to zero, you will be in a deep and total trance. Do you understand?"

"Yes," said Mrs. White.

"Three . . . two . . . one . . . zero."

Mrs. White sat very still, her eyes closed.

"You can open your eyes," the guest told her.

The maid obeyed. Her eyes were dark, glassy, blank.

"Good," said the hypnotist. "Now listen to me and listen well. From now on, whenever you hear the word 'Candlestick' you will return to this state of trance. Do you understand?"

"Yes."

"What is the word?"

"Candlestick," said Mrs. White.

"Right. When you hear the word 'Candlestick' you must do the next thing you are told. You are not to question it. Just do it."

"Candlestick."

"Yes. Then, when you hear the word 'Rope,' you will come out of the trance. You will not remember anything that has happened. Do you understand?"

"I understand."

"Good," said the hypnotist, glancing at the door again. "Rope!"

Mrs. White blinked and looked around the

Kitchen, confused. "Will you look at me?" she said. "Just sitting around the Kitchen chatting with one of the guests. As if Mr. Boddy doesn't have company!"

"Oh now," said the guest, "you're allowed a little break now and then."

Mrs. White picked up a tray containing slices of pumpkin pie. "Here," said the guest with a smile. "Let me help you with that."

The guest followed Mrs. White into the Library, where they rejoined the party.

Mr. Boddy raised his glass of lemonade. "Ladies and gentlemen," he cried. "I'd like to make a toast. To my new Persian statuette. And — to all of you. I couldn't enjoy this occasion without you! You know, something tells me that this weekend is going to be our best weekend here, ever."

He was wrong. But it was one of the strangest weekends the guests had ever spent at the Boddy mansion. Every time one of the guests mentioned the word "Candlestick," Mrs. White began acting peculiar.

Later that night, for instance, Mrs. White over-heard a guest talk about buying a new Candlestick. Then she heard another guest telling someone to "Go jump in the lake."

Mrs. White dropped her silver tray and marched straight out of the house. The guests ran after her. But she walked right up to the Boddy Pond and jumped in!

At breakfast the next morning, she heard a guest complimenting Mr. Boddy on his beautiful gold Candlestick. Then she heard another guest say, "Please pass me the mustard."

She walked straight to Colonel Mustard and tried to drag him out of his seat.

Finally, on Saturday night, the hypnotist approached her in the Ball Room. "Candlestick," whispered the guest.

Mrs. White's eyes went dark, glassy, blank.

"Well," said the hypnotist, "you've been making a fine mess of things, haven't you? You're only supposed to go into a trance when *I* say the word 'Candlestick.' But never mind. This will all be over soon.

"Tonight," continued the hypnotist, "you will steal Mr. Boddy's Persian statuette. You will mail it to this address."

The hypnotist slipped a piece of paper into the pocket of the maid's apron. "And then you will eat that piece of paper. And forget the whole thing ever happened. Understood?"

"Yes."

"Good . . . Rope!"

Who put the spell on Mrs. White in the Kitchen?

You can rule out only one of the following: Colonel Mustard and Mr. Green.

You can also rule out at least two of the following: Mrs. White, Colonel Mustard, and Mrs. Peacock.

And you can rule out one of the following (one you haven't already ruled out as a suspect): Mrs. White or Mrs. Peacock.

WHO HYPNOTIZED MRS. WHITE?

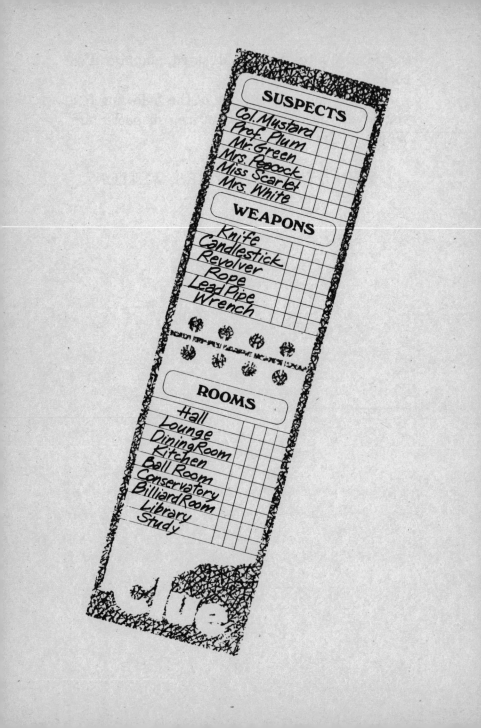

SOLUTION

MR. GREEN in the KITCHEN with CANDLESTICK and ROPE as his passwords.

If Colonel Mustard did it, we would have to rule out Mrs. White and Mrs. Peacock. But the final clue forces us to rule out one or the other of those two — and we must rule out a suspect whom we hadn't ruled out already.

That means the second clue ruled out Mustard. And thanks to our first clue, that leaves Green. The other guests didn't know it, but Mr. Green was reading a book on hypnosis just before coming to Boddy's for the weekend. And now he's the proud owner of a priceless Persian statuette.

12.
April Fools

"BY THE WAY," MR. BODDY TOLD HIS five dinner guests. "I'm afraid I have some bad news. Due to a tragic mix-up, no dessert will be served tonight!"

Mr. Boddy looked around the dinner table with obvious delight. Then he burst out laughing.

"April Fools!" he roared.

His guests stared at him blankly.

"Boy, did I have you all going. You should have seen the looks on your faces!"

"We sure were surprised," agreed Mr. Green, looking very bored.

"I think I fainted," said Mrs. Peacock.

"I had a heart attack," said Professor Plum.

"Ha ha ha!" laughed Boddy. "Well, I know it was naughty of me. But I think it's important to have a little fun now and then. And now —" He tinkled a tiny silver dinner bell. "I'll have Mrs. White bring in your real and very delicious dessert . . . baked Alaska!"

Everyone oohed and ahhed politely. Then Colonel Mustard said, "By the way, Miss Scarlet, you ate your pheasant with the wrong fork."

Miss Scarlet instantly turned the color of her name. "I beg your pardon?"

"Yes, I couldn't help noticing you ate your pheasant with the small fork." He held up his own small fork to show her. "This is the salad fork. The big fork is the fork you should use for main courses like pheasant."

"Why, Colonel Mustard, you ignorant cad," Miss Scarlet flashed back. "I guess you didn't know that pheasant is the one exception to that rule. Pheasant is always eaten with the small fork."

Mr. Boddy rang the bell again, nervously. "Well," he said, "let's not be unpleasant about a pheasant." He tinkled the bell harder. "I can't imagine where Mrs. White is. She had the dessert all prepared in a big silver dish."

"You don't mean *that* silver dish, do you?" Mr. Green pointed to a large silver dish, covered with a large silver lid. It was sitting right by Mr. Boddy's elbow.

"Oh, my goodness!" said Mr. Boddy. "Yes! This is our baked Alaska dessert. Mrs. White must have brought it out when I wasn't looking. If I could have everyone's attention."

He put a hand on the handle of the lid.

"Drumroll please," said Mr. Boddy.

Mr. Green drummed on the table with his hands. Then Mr. Boddy pulled off the lid with a flourish.

Revealing . . .

Mrs. White's head.

The head sat on a bed of lettuce. The mouth was wide open, and stuffed with an apple.

Mr. Boddy gasped. Colonel Mustard choked. Professor Plum screamed. Miss Scarlet fainted into Professor Plum's arms. So did Mrs. Peacock. The two banged into each other and fell to the floor.

Mr. Green laughed. He reached over and plucked out the apple.

"April Fools!" shouted Mrs. White's head. Then she pulled her head down through a hole that had been secretly cut in the tray. Soon, she appeared above the table again, all in one piece.

There was a stunned silence. Then everyone burst into applause. "Mr. Green helped me rig it," Mrs. White said shyly. Then she turned around and rolled her eyes.

Which was when the lights went off.

There were screams.

When the lights came back on, Miss Scarlet and Mrs. Peacock both fainted again. Professor Plum lay slumped in his chair. He had a knife stuck in his head. He was dead.

Then he sat up straight again. "Just kidding," he said. "April Fools!"

"Oh, my!" Mr. Boddy said. "You people are just too good at this. Wow!" He felt his heart. "Good, still beating! And now that we've all had our excitement for the year, Mrs. White, if you would be so kind. The baked Alaska?"

"Certainly," Mrs. White said.

"Don't forget," Colonel Mustard told Miss Scarlet with a smile, "you eat the dessert with the little spoon."

"The large spoon, you big brute!" cried Miss Scarlet.

"The little spoon!"

"The big spoon!"

Soon, they were shouting at each other at the top of their lungs. Then, Miss Scarlet slapped Colonel Mustard with all her might. The Colonel looked stunned. Then he grabbed the Lead Pipe and chased Miss Scarlet around the table in a circle.

Everyone was screaming for him to stop.

But he didn't. Miss Scarlet slipped and slid into a corner. Colonel Mustard stood over her with the pipe. His arm came up. It went down fast. There was a dull, horrible thud.

The other guests rushed forward.

But they were too late.

Miss Scarlet lay dead at the Colonel's feet. Around her limp body, a pool of dark red blood was slowly spreading.

"I'll call a doctor," cried Professor Plum, who

still had the Knife in his head. He picked up Miss Scarlet's body and rushed from the room. Mr. Boddy staggered around the room clutching his heart. Mrs. Peacock and Mrs. White followed him around in a circle, screaming.

Mr. Green seized Colonel Mustard. "You're under arrest," yelled Green.

"What?" cried Mustard. "You dare to touch me?" He slapped Green in the face with his glove. "I challenge you to a duel!"

He raised the Lead Pipe high in the air. Mr. Green pulled out the Candlestick. And they began to fence. Colonel Mustard swung hard with the Lead Pipe. Mr. Green ducked. Mustard shattered a wall mirror.

Mr. Green swung back with the Candlestick. He smashed a wall lamp.

Huddled in a corner, Mr. Boddy, Mrs. White, and Mrs. Peacock begged the two men to stop. But Mustard kept stalking Green around the table. He swung the Lead Pipe again and again. Green held the Candlestick with two hands, blocking the blows.

Then Mustard swung one more time.

This time Green stepped out of the way.

And as Mustard went flying by, Green clonked him on the head with the Candlestick. The Lead Pipe dropped to the floor. Followed by the Colonel.

Mrs. Peacock ran to the Colonel's side. She

90

knelt down and lifted Mustard's wrist. She felt for his pulse. When she looked up, she had tears in her eyes. "He's dead," she said.

Mr. Boddy and Mrs. White ran from the room in horror.

And Mrs. Peacock let go of Mustard's wrist.

It stayed up in the air.

Mrs. Peacock was laughing now. So was Mr. Green. And so was Colonel Mustard.

"Yes, doctor," the Professor said into the phone in the Lounge. "Mr. Boddy's mansion. And please hurry. Miss Scarlet may only have seconds to live!"

A long hand with shiny red nails tapped his shoulder.

"Just a second, Miss Scarlet," Plum told the woman. "I'm on the phone with the doctor."

He thought about this for a moment. Then he said into the phone, "Hold on a second." He looked back at Miss Scarlet. Then he screamed.

"April Fools," she said, hanging up the phone.

The door flew open. "Colonel Mustard — he's dead," Mr. Boddy gasped.

Then he saw Miss Scarlet and let out a scream.

"Yes," said Plum. "It turns out the joke was on us. She's fine after all." He pulled out a Revolver. He pointed it at the woman in red. "That was some joke," he said. "Why would you want to make saps out of us? Don't you know I've killed people for less?"

Miss Scarlet began to shake.

"Oh, no, please, Professor," begged Mr. Boddy, dropping to his knees. "Don't shoot her!"

Professor Plum laughed. "Scared you, didn't I, Miss Scarlet? Now you know what it feels like. April Fools!"

BANG!

The Revolver went off accidentally. Miss Scarlet crumpled to the floor.

"Whoops," said Plum.

Mr. Boddy ran to her side.

Around her limp body, a pool of dark red blood was slowly spreading.

"Oh, speak to me, speak to me," pleaded Mr. Boddy.

Miss Scarlet's eyes fluttered. Her lips moved.

"Oh, Miss Scarlet, can you hear me? It's me, Boddy."

"Mr. Boddy," she said, ever so quietly. "I . . ."

He leaned closer. Her voice grew fainter:

"I just want you to know . . ."

He leaned closer.

". . . that . . ."

He put his ear right up to Miss Scarlet's red lips.

And then he heard her dying words:

"APRIL FOOLS!" she shouted right in his ear.

Professor Plum and Miss Scarlet were chortling happily. Mr. Boddy fainted again.

"Oh dear," Plum said.

Miss Scarlet knelt down next to Boddy and began slapping his cheeks. When they got him back on his feet, there was a horrible crash and scream from the Ball Room.

Professor Plum raced out. Followed by Miss Scarlet and a tottering Mr. Boddy.

In the Ball Room, Mrs. White stood frozen in fright.

Her hands clutched her face, her mouth was open in a silent scream. At her feet lay an overturned silver tray and a mess of broken teacups. Across the room lay Mrs. Peacock.

Mrs. Peacock was not a pretty sight. Her limbs lay at lifeless angles, blood covered her face and clotted her hair. And next to her head was the Wrench.

"I found her like this," Mrs. White stuttered.

"Is she really dead?" Plum asked her.

"Take a look," cried Mrs. White.

The other guests gathered around, staring down in horror at the grisly sight.

"This is what comes from too much April Fooling," Miss Scarlet said gravely.

"Yes," said Boddy, "I should never have lied about there not being any dessert."

The gags they had just pulled raced through

each guest's mind: Mr. Green helping Mrs. White put her head on the tray. Professor Plum putting the Knife in his head. Colonel Mustard and Miss Scarlet faking her murder. Mr. Green and Colonel Mustard faking a duel to the death, with Mrs. Peacock's help. Plum and Miss Scarlet staging a fake shooting.

With Mrs. Peacock dead at their feet, these practical jokes sure seemed in poor taste.

"Well," said Miss Scarlet. "It seems that one of us is a murderer. And no fooling."

EXCEPT FOR THE REAL VICTIM AND THE REAL KILLER, EACH GUEST WAS INVOLVED IN TWO GAGS. AS ALWAYS, MR. BODDY IS NOT A SUSPECT. SO . . . WHO KILLED MRS. PEACOCK?

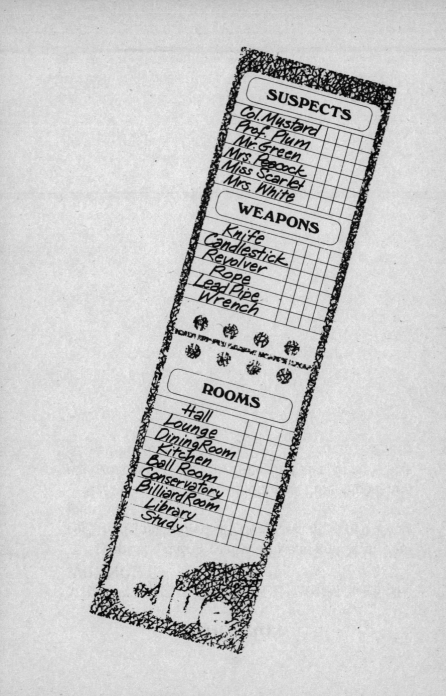

96

SOLUTION

MRS. WHITE in the BALL ROOM with the
WRENCH

Except she didn't really. For she and Mrs. Peacock had just pulled off their second April Fools
joke.

Mrs. Peacock washed off the fake blood and
everyone went back to dinner. At last, Mrs. White
served her baked Alaska.

13.
Who Killed Mr. Boddy?

MR. BODDY WAS LAUGHING MERRILY. He couldn't stop.

It was just too wonderful.

Here he was, in the Dining Room of his priceless mansion, surrounded by his favorite guests. They were so charming, so warm, so friendly.

Mrs. White was serving another delicious dinner.

Everything was perfect.

Mr. Boddy tapped on his wine glass with a knife. "My friends," he said. "My dear, dear friends. I hate to interrupt this wonderful dinner party even for an instant. But I have an important announcement to make. You, too, Mrs. White," he said.

Mrs. White was halfway out the door. She was making an angry face. But when she came back into the room, she was smiling. "Me, too?"

"Yes. What I want to say," Mr. Boddy began, "is that . . . that I can't tell you how fond I've become of all of you."

"Here, here," said Colonel Mustard, applauding.

Mr. Boddy waved his hand for silence.

"I guess a lot of people would envy me, being a multibillionaire and all. I live in this famous mansion in a pretty town. But it would be awfully lonely living here, awfully lonely . . . except for all of you."

He beamed across the table at Miss Scarlet. Miss Scarlet dabbed her lips with a red napkin and batted her eyes.

"We've had some wild times, haven't we?" he said with a chuckle. "I know, I know, sometimes things have gotten a little nasty."

"Mr. Boddy!" said a shocked Mrs. Peacock. "Watch your language."

"Sorry. But through it all, through it all, we've stayed friends, haven't we?"

"Quite so!" said Professor Plum, raising his glass.

"Yes, after my beloved wife Bessie Boddy died . . ." Mr. Boddy paused for a moment. His eyes watered. "I never thought I could be happy again. But you've changed that. You've kept me so busy on so many dark, lonely nights."

"You've been a busy Boddy," joked Mr. Green.

Mr. Boddy laughed louder than anyone else. "A busy Boddy! Excellent! Yes!"

Then he grew serious again. "So," he said, "here's what I wanted to tell you. Last night I made out a new will."

There was utter silence at the table. All eyes were fixed on Mr. Boddy.

"As you know, there is no living heir to the Boddy fortune. If I die, I want you all to know that I've provided for each of you. Yes, I have instructed my lawyers to divide my billions evenly among the six of you."

"Awfully nice of you," stammered Mrs. White.

"And I've left this mansion to the six of you, as well. So that you can continue our wonderful tradition of these get-togethers even after I'm gone."

"How lovely," murmured Mrs. Peacock.

"Now, don't be alarmed, any of you," added Mr. Boddy with a laugh, "I'm not planning on dying for a very, very, *very* long time!"

Mr. Boddy was dead the next morning.

His body was found lying facedown in the Library. Beside him lay the murder weapon: the Wrench.

The police were called. They outlined the body with chalk. Then an ambulance took the body away.

The six suspects were told to wait in the Conservatory.

"This is so horrible," wept Mrs. White. "One of you is a murderer!"

"I see," said Mr. Green. "And you're innocent?"

Mrs. White looked shocked. "I loved Mr. Boddy," she said. Behind her hanky she stuck out her tongue.

"We all loved him," said Miss Scarlet. "But we all love money, too."

"It's true," said Professor Plum. "Any one of us could have done it. We all have the same motive."

"Were you in the Library last night, Professor?" Mrs. Peacock asked him.

"Yes. But only to borrow a book on butterfly collecting. Mr. Boddy was alive and well at the time. I might add, I was there before you, Mrs. Peacock."

"Well!" snapped Mrs. Peacock, "Mr. Green was in the Library after me."

"And Professor Plum was in the Library after me," said Mrs. White.

"I was in the Library before Mrs. White," said Miss Scarlet.

"I was in the Library before Mr. Green," said Colonel Mustard.

"And so the murderer," said the Professor, "must have been the suspect who was in the Library last."

WHO KILLED MR. BODDY?

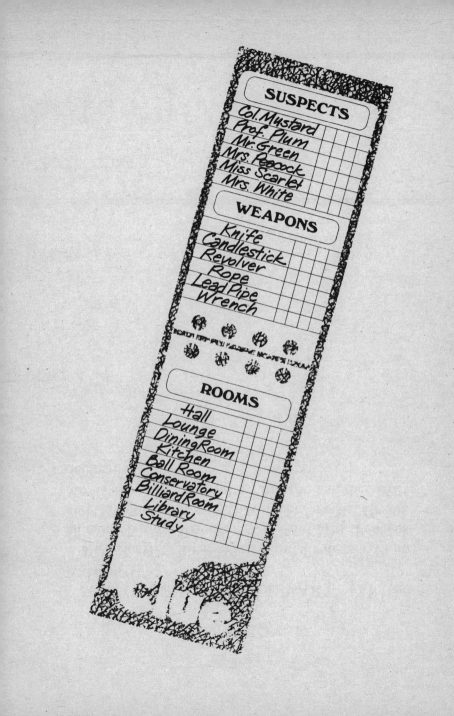

SOLUTION

MR. GREEN in the LIBRARY with the WRENCH

Miss Scarlet, Mrs. White, and Professor Plum all came before Mrs. Peacock. And Mrs. Peacock and Colonel Mustard both came before Mr. Green. Mr. Green was last and committed the dastardly deed.